Zoomer

WRITTEN & ILLUSTRATED BY

NED YOUNG

SCHOLASTIC INC.
New York Toronto London Auckland
Sydney Mexico City New Delhi Hong Kong

A big thank-you to Zoomer's groomer, Maria Modugno

ISBN 978-0-545-34021-2

12 11 10 9 8 7 6 5 4 3 2   11 12 13 14 15 16/0

Printed in the U.S.A.   08

This edition first printing, January 2011

Typography by Dana Fritts

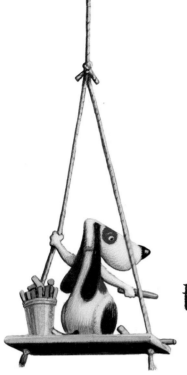

For Melanie and our three free spirits,
Erin, James, and Kevin, who make life
a wondrous adventure

And to Mom and Dad for the
constant supply of crayons

"Wake up, Dad!" shouted Cooper as he caught a fly ball. "You're missing the game!"

Dad's pillow had become home plate even though neither the sun nor Dad was up yet.

"Okay, pups. Time to get ready for school," announced Dad, wondering if he would be able to get the kids out the door on time while Mom was away.

The twins, Hooper and Cooper, made their beds. But Zoomer—*boing, boing, boing*—was bouncing up and down on his.

"Zoomer," said Hooper, "what do you think you're doing?"

"I'm not Zoomer," said Zoomer in a superhero voice. "I'm Power Puppy!"

"Well, whoever you are," said Cooper, "you'd better get ready for school."

"I'm not going to school today," announced Zoomer. "I'm way too busy."

"Yeah, right," said Hooper.

"Yeah, good luck with that," said Cooper, and they both burst out laughing.

"What would you boys like for breakfast?" called Dad.

"Nachos," yipped Hooper.

"Chili dogs," barked Cooper.

"Very funny," said Dad. "I don't think so. Hey, where's Zoomer?"

"He says he's not going to school today," said Cooper.

"He's waaaaay too busy," added Hooper.

Just then . . .

"Pretty cool, huh?" said Zoomer.
"Well, it certainly is LOUD," said Dad. "Come
on—all three of you—back upstairs to take a bath."
"Yeah!" exclaimed Zoomer. "I love bubbles."

Dad was putting breakfast on the table when
Hooper announced, "Zoomer's going for a world
record and won't share any bubble bath."
"A world record in what?" asked Dad hesitantly.

"Blowing the world's biggest bubble!" replied Hooper.

Dad took a photograph to document Zoomer's accomplishment and reminded the pups to finish their bath and put on clean collars.

As Dad was packing their lunch boxes, Cooper
tattled, "Da-ad, Zoomer's playing with his food."

"You know," said Dad to Zoomer, "the *sandbox* would be a better place to build things."

"Wow! That's a *great* idea!" whooped Zoomer.

"But right now," coaxed Dad, "you need to get ready for school."

"No, thank you," said Zoomer politely. "I won't be going to school today." And off he ran.

"I think that kid needs a major time-out," said Hooper. Cooper nodded in agreement.

"Hey, Dad!" yelled Zoomer. "Do we have any more sand? I think my brontosaurus would like a little brother."

"Not now," said Dad. "You need to get ready for school."
"I can't," shouted Zoomer. "I have a very full schedule today."

While Hooper and Cooper were brushing their teeth, combing their hair, and practicing spelling words . . . Zoomer sailed a pirate ship . . .

Drew a picture of the universe . . .

And performed a magic trick.

POOF!

Then Zoomer persuaded some birds
to help him launch his rocket ship.

"I don't know what to do," said Dad, walking the twins to the bus stop. "I'm in charge and I can't figure Zoomer out. He's never acted this way before."

"Ground him!" said Hooper.

"For a month!" added Cooper.

Dad just shook his head and counted the days until Mom would be back.

Meanwhile, the rocket ship made a beautiful
landing, and Zoomer proceeded to explore a strange
world where everything was slanted.

"Greetings, inhabitants of the roof,"
declared Zoomer. "I come in peace."
The birds looked puzzled.

Zoomer's rocket ship landed back on earth right near the bus stop.

"AAAAAH! Martians!" screamed Hooper.

"Save us! Save us!" yelped Cooper.

Just then Zoomer emerged with a big grin.

"Zoomer, I don't understand," said Dad. "You've always liked school. Why don't you want to go today?"

"BECAUSE, YOU SILLY EARTHLINGS,"
said Zoomer into his microphone,
"TODAY IS . . ."

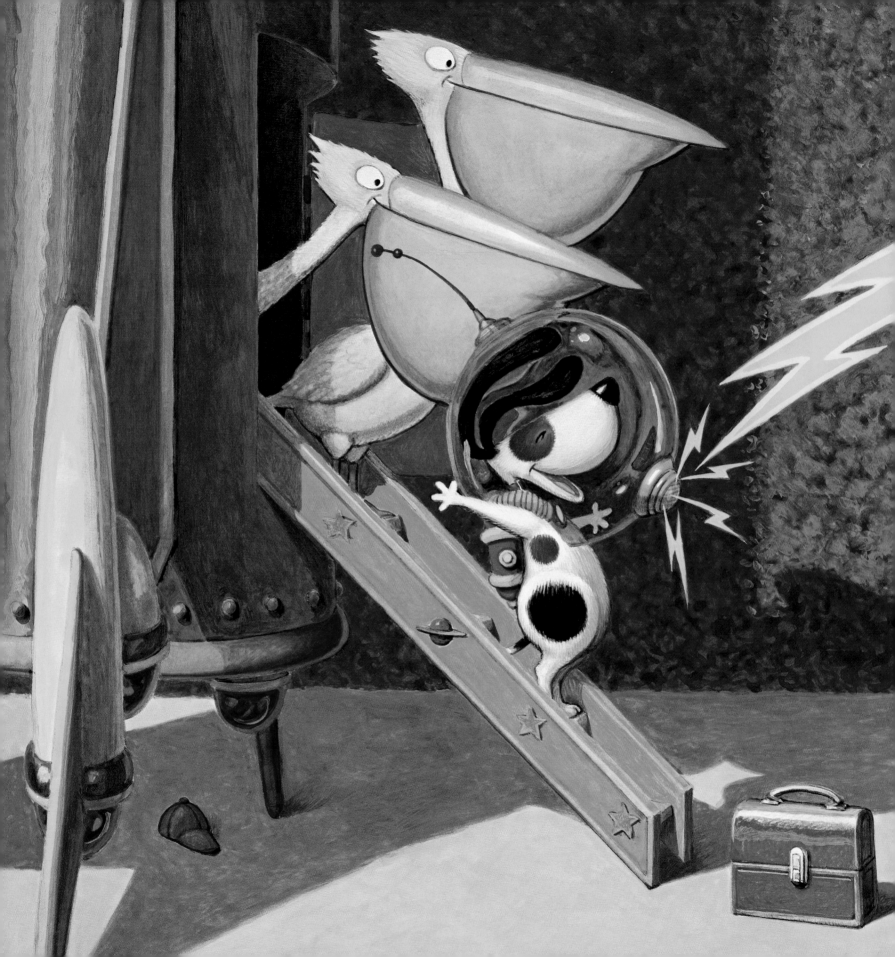